J
JOH

Johnston, Louisa M
    A Monkey in the family; by Louisa M. Johnston and Mabel
Cameron Bristle. Illus. by Lois Axeman.   Albert Whitman
© 1972

    128p illus   3.50

    Mid was the monkey's first name, but her middle name was
mischief. Nothing at the Bristol house was the same after Mid
joined the family. "What next?" the five girls asked as Mid upset
the basement, teased the cat and dog, and startled the neighbors.
Lovable and funny, Mid was always forgiven.

1 Monkeys—Stories   I Title

A Monkey in the Family

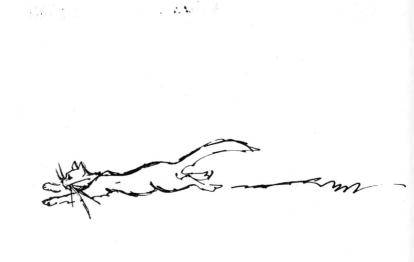

A Monkey in the Family

Louisa M. Johnston
and Mabel Cameron Bristle

Illustrated by Lois Axeman

ALBERT WHITMAN & *Company, Chicago*

ISBN 0–8075–5256–9
LIBRARY OF CONGRESS CATALOG CARD 73–188431
TEXT © 1972 BY ALBERT WHITMAN & COMPANY
ILLUSTRATIONS © 1972 BY ALBERT WHITMAN & COMPANY
PUBLISHED SIMULTANEOUSLY IN CANADA BY
GEORGE J. MCLEOD, LIMITED, TORONTO
PRINTED IN THE U.S.A.

To my daughters, Louise, Jean, Barbara, "Tim," and Nancy, and to my grandchildren and great-grandchildren.

Mabel Cameron Bristle

Did It All Happen?

Was Mid a real monkey? Did she do the funny things that happen in this book?

Yes, Mid was a real monkey, and she belonged to Mabel Cameron Bristle's family. As in the story, Barbara brought a little monkey home. But the time was a good many years ago. Now Barbara and her sisters are grown and have families of their own. And nothing has pleased their children more than to hear stories about Mid.

One day Mrs. Bristle decided to write notes about all Mid's funny adventures. She hoped to keep her plans for a book a secret from her daughters, and she almost did, but not quite.

Now, with the help of coauthor Louisa Johnston, Mid's story is for many children to enjoy. And all the fun is true, except for the time when Mid had her picture taken. But it isn't fair to tell more here. Mid's story is too much fun to spoil.

Mabel Cameron Brittle

Evanston, Illinois

CONTENTS

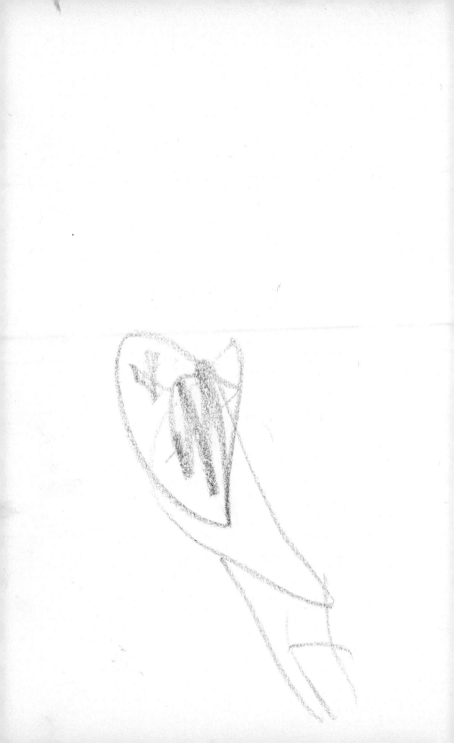

1 Surprise for the Bristols

Everyone looked at Barbara. No one said a thing. This never happened in the Bristol house—the seven Bristols always had a lot to say at dinnertime. Why was everyone so quiet?

It was because Barbara, the middle one of the five girls, was in the middle of something. Something new and exciting. Her sisters were sure of it. So were Mr. and Mrs. Bristol.

Barbara looked around at her family. She gulped. "There's something I want to ask all of you. A surprise," she said and stopped. She was sure her big sisters were thinking, "What silly idea does Barbara have now?"

Mrs. Bristol smiled and said, "Go on, Barbara. What is it?"

"Something happened at the pet store today."

Louise, the oldest of the girls, asked, "What's the surprise about that? Something has happened every day since you've been helping there."

"Did the rabbits get out?" asked Nancy. She was the baby of the family.

"No, but there was a fire."

"A fire!" cried Mrs. Bristol. "Oh, Barbara!"

Mr. Bristol asked, "Was anyone hurt? What about the animals?"

Barbara shook her head. "No one was hurt. But—but some of the animals need homes. Please, Mom, may we take a monkey—just a little monkey?"

A monkey! All the Bristols looked at each other and then at Mrs. Bristol. This time Barbara was asking too much! Mrs. Bristol would never let her keep a monkey —or would she?

Mrs. Bristol's answer was quick. She smiled. "Yes, Barbara, we can. It sounds funny. But I've always wanted a monkey. And here is the chance."

Barbara jumped up and hugged her mother. Mr. Bristol laughed. Louise, Jean, Tim (her real name was Margaret), and Nancy all began to talk at once.

"Mother! What are you thinking? A monkey, of all things!" Louise said. She was always the practical big sister.

Jean asked, "How will Pat and Kelly feel? Will a cat and dog and monkey all live in the same house?"

"Will they fight?" asked Nancy.

"That's enough," said Mr. Bristol. "Your mother says yes. We'll give the monkey a

14

home. When will you bring it, Barbara?"

Barbara looked around the table and smiled. Was it true? They were going to give the monkey a home? Her idea was not too silly after all.

"She's here now," Barbara told her father. "She's in a box on the porch. I hoped Mom would say yes. And she did."

"Here now?" Nancy asked. "Oh, Barbara!"

The Bristols gave each other what Tim called their leave-it-to-Barbara look. Barbara's ideas always took in the whole family.

"Come and meet her," Barbara said. "I know you'll like Mid. You'll be glad I brought her home."

The family followed Barbara to the back porch. She held up a large hatbox. There were holes in the box to let in air.

Barbara lifted off the box top. "Here she is. Here's Mid."

15

Seven pairs of eyes looked down into the hatbox. At the very bottom of the box was a small monkey.

The monkey did not move. It did not look up. It just curled itself into a ball. It looked sad and helpless.

"You poor little thing!" Mrs. Bristol exclaimed.

"She's afraid," Barbara said. "First there was the fire. Now there are a lot of strange people. She'll be all right when she feels at home."

Barbara picked up the monkey. It was almost like a baby. But it looked happier in Barbara's arms.

"She's cute," Nancy said, wishing she could hold the little monkey.

"Why is she named Mid?" asked Jean.

"We called her Mid for the Midway Pet Shop," Barbara said. "Mid just seemed a good name for her."

"It could be Mid for middle," Louise

16

said. "I think she's going to be just like you, Barbara—always in the middle of everything."

"Have you thought about where Mid is going to stay?" asked Mr. Bristol.

Barbara had thought perhaps she could keep Mid in the room she shared with Tim and Nancy. But she was pretty sure that wasn't such a good idea. Her father would not like it.

None of the Bristols knew anything about monkeys and how to take care of them. Barbara had only worked at the pet shop for a week. She hadn't learned much about monkeys in that time.

Mrs. Bristol helped Barbara out. She said, "I think Mid will be safe in the basement tonight. I don't think she can get out."

"That sounds good," Mr. Bristol agreed. "In the morning we can find a better place for her."

With Barbara going first, the Bristols made a parade down to the basement.

Kelly, the Bristols' old dog, stood at the top of the steps and wagged his tail. Something new was going on, he seemed to know, but he was not part of it.

Pat, the blue-eyed white cat, didn't pay any attention at all. He was always like that.

"Mid needs a box to sleep in," Louise said.

Barbara smiled—even Louise liked Mid.

Nancy ran upstairs. She came back with a doll blanket. "Here, Mid needs a soft bed."

Jean folded the blanket and tucked it into the box Louise had found.

Tim hunted in the kitchen for something. She came back with a small dish. "Mid will need water," she said.

Mrs. Bristol looked around the tidy basement. She wanted to choose a good place for Mid's box. "In the morning we'll find out more about what she needs," Mrs. Bristol said.

"Mid should have a swing," said Mr. Bristol. "I'm sure of that. I'll make her one in the morning."

Already Mid seemed like part of the family.

2 What a Mess!

Before she went upstairs to bed, Mrs. Bristol stood by the basement door. There was no sound.

"That little monkey is asleep," she said to herself. She smiled. Maybe it was odd for her to want a monkey. But she always had. And now there was one, right here in the family.

The house was quiet. All the girls were asleep. Mr. Bristol came along and asked, "So you think Mid is safe? I wonder when monkeys wake up."

"I guess monkeys wake up when people do," Mrs. Bristol said.

"Well, if she wakes up early, I hope she keeps away from my tools."

Mrs. Bristol laughed. "I don't think a little monkey can hurt your workbench. Most of your tools are bigger than she is."

Mr. Bristol said, "That's true." But he sounded as if he was not so sure about what Mid could do.

Mr. Bristol worked at home. He made plans for houses, schools, and stores. He was a good architect. But when he was tired of plans, he liked to make something with his tools in the basement.

Barbara was the first of the Bristols to wake up the next morning. She couldn't wait for anyone else. She wanted to find out how Mid was. After all, she was the one who had brought the little monkey home.

Barbara hurried downstairs. She could

not hear a sound from the basement. That was good.

Slowly, carefully, Barbara opened the basement door. She didn't want Mid to run into the kitchen.

Barbara looked down the stairs. She could not believe her eyes. She did not know what to think. No Mid was in sight. Her bed was empty.

"Mid!" Barbara cried. "You naughty monkey! Where are you?"

Just then Mrs. Bristol called, "Barbara, are you all right?" She hurried down the stairs.

One look, and Mrs. Bristol exclaimed, "Oh, Barbara, what will we do? I never saw anything like this in all my life!"

The Bristols' clean, neat basement was a mess. It looked like a monkey's playground. There was soap all over the floor. There were clean clothes pulled out of a basket.

Mr. Bristol's tools were on the floor by his workbench. Sawdust was scattered around. Some paint was spilled.

Barbara said over and over, "How did she do it? How did one little monkey do all this?"

"I don't think Mid slept a wink all night," Mrs. Bristol said. "Where can she be?"

Nancy heard her mother and Barbara. She came downstairs. She took a look, then she began to laugh. There was such a mess!

"It isn't funny, Nancy," Mrs. Bristol said. "And we can't find Mid anywhere."

"Please, Nancy, help us look," Barbara said.

So Nancy looked low, Barbara looked high, and Mrs. Bristol looked in the middle. But nobody could see Mid.

Barbara was calling, "Mid, where are you?" as Mr. Bristol came downstairs.

"Well!" he said. "Who wanted a monkey in the family?"

Mrs. Bristol sighed. "I did. But I guess I didn't know a thing about monkeys."

Mr. Bristol picked up a can of paint and a screwdriver. "I know one thing. Your little monkey has to have a home. A home spelled c-a-g-e, where she can't get into trouble. You are looking at someone who's going to be the first monkey architect."

"Oh, Daddy!" Barbara cried. "You're so good not to get cross."

"What good would it do?" Mr. Bristol asked. "Besides, I'm glad that it wasn't an elephant you brought home."

Louise called down, "What about breakfast? I have to go to work."

Jean said, "I've put the eggs on."

"Mid has to be here somewhere," Mrs. Bristol said. "The windows are shut. I'm sure she hasn't had a chance to run upstairs. Let's go and eat."

"We'll feel better," Mr. Bristol agreed.

Barbara said, "Mom, Mid has me in the middle of lots of trouble. I'll clean up the basement after breakfast."

Mrs. Bristol smiled at Barbara. "We'll clean it up," she said.

"And I'll find Mid," Nancy promised.

The back door shut. Louise and Jean were off for work. They would be gone all day.

Mrs. Bristol and Barbara looked at each other. It was going to be a busy day at home.

"I know where I am going to begin," Mr. Bristol said. "I'll see you at lunchtime."

"But—," Mrs. Bristol began, "I thought that—"

"You thought I was going to help. I am helping. In my way. You'll see."

And Mr. Bristol took a notebook and went out the back door. Then he came back.

26

He asked, "Have you seen Kelly and Pat? I think that dog and cat know something is going on. They don't like it."

Mrs. Bristol said, "I let them out when I came downstairs. But I haven't seen them after that. Oh, dear! They can't be lost, too."

Barbara had an idea. She said, "Dad, I'll get Kelly's food dish. You whistle for him. Maybe he and Pat want to be asked— you know, they think we aren't taking care of them this morning."

"Maybe you're right," Mr. Bristol agreed.

He went to the back door. He had his own way of calling the pets. He could only whistle one thing. It was "Bobwhite," just like the bird call.

Now Mr. Bristol whistled "Bobwhite! Bobwhite!" and waited. Then he tried again. Sure enough, there came Kelly, but no Pat.

Barbara put the dog dish down by the back step. And which pet got there first? Pat! That cat was always faster than Kelly. But there was always enough for both pets, and Barbara called, "Here, Pat, here's your dish."

"At least two of our pets are here," Mr. Bristol said. "Too bad I can't whistle for Mid. But you girls have good eyes. You'll find her. See you at lunchtime." And he was gone.

"Come on, Nancy," Barbara called. "Come on, Tim. Help me find Mid."

"I'll clean up the kitchen," Mrs. Bristol decided. "You girls will be better at monkey finding than I'd be."

"We have to find her," Barbara said. "Poor Mid. She hasn't even had breakfast."

"Yes, poor Mid," Mrs. Bristol said. "Good luck."

"I'll look around the stairs and Daddy's

workbench," Tim offered.

Barbara said, "I'll look around the washing machine. Oh, what a mess!"

"I'll just look everywhere," Nancy said.

"You're my littlest sister and biggest helper," Barbara teased.

After a while Tim asked, "Are you sure Mid is here? We've looked and looked. Did she get out?"

But Barbara felt sure Mid was in the basement. "She's so small and quick. And there are so many places for a monkey to hide. That's the trouble."

"What about Kelly?" Nancy asked. "We could let him sniff Mid's blanket. Then he could find her."

"I don't think Kelly's that kind of dog," Barbara answered. She felt tired and cross. Where could Mid be?

Barbara sat down on the bottom basement step. She leaned back to rest. Then she saw something. It looked like a rope hanging down from a furnace pipe.

It looked like a rope, but it moved. It moved like—like a tail! Like a monkey's tail. And that was what it was.

Barbara would have jumped up. But she remembered just in time. At the pet shop she had learned you have to move slowly around animals. You have to be quiet.

Very slowly Barbara turned her head and looked up. Two brown eyes looked down at her.

Now Barbara lifted one arm slowly. Oh, if only Tim and Nancy didn't scare Mid.

Tim saw Mid next. She saw Barbara lifting her arm slowly. Tim put her hand over her mouth. She didn't make a sound. She backed out of the way and whispered to Nancy.

Nothing moved in the basement. It was very quiet.

"Mid," Barbara called softly. "It's all right, Mid. Be a good girl. Come to me."

30

Mid didn't move. She looked at Barbara.

Barbara sat still. She called quietly, "Mid, Mid."

Then all at once something brown and small flew through the air. Mid dropped down from the furnace pipe, right into Barbara's lap. Two little brown arms hugged Barbara around the neck.

"Why, she's scared," Tim whispered.

Barbara petted the monkey. "You'd be scared too if a lot of big giants were hunting for you," she said.

3 A Monkey House

Nancy ran up the steps to the kitchen.

"Mom, we found Mid! She's all right. Barbara has her."

Mrs. Bristol put down the cup she was washing, dried her hands, and hurried down to the basement.

Barbara was still petting Mid and talking softly to her. She looked up and smiled at her mother.

How could anyone be cross with such a little thing, smaller than a baby? Mrs. Bristol couldn't be.

32

"Oh, you funny little thing," she said. Very gently Barbara put Mid in her mother's arms. Mid seemed to feel the safety and love there. She didn't try to get away.

"She's quite tame," Barbara explained. "And I guess she's tired."

"She must be hungry. What does she eat?" Tim asked.

"Oh," Barbara exclaimed. "I forgot. She must be starved. I have some food from the pet store. It was all I could save, not much—"

"Never mind," Mrs. Bristol said. "We'll give it to her now. But she has to stay in the hatbox. She can't tear up the basement again."

Nancy touched Mid with one finger. But Mid didn't seem to like that and Nancy stopped.

"Such a funny little face," she said. "Are you sure she's a girl? She looks like a little old man."

Mrs. Bristol laughed. "Barbara says she's a girl. And what else can we have but girls in this family? Except for Pat and Kelly, of course."

Barbara came back with a dish of food for Mid. She lifted Mid into the hatbox and put the lid on it.

"I'm afraid to make the holes too big to let in light," she said. "Mid could get out."

"If it's dark in the box, she may sleep," Mrs. Bristol said.

Nancy had an idea. She ran upstairs and was soon back. She had a birdcage.

"How about this?" she asked.

But Barbara shook her head. "That cage is too small. It's a good idea, but Mid could hardly turn around in it. Oh, dear."

"I have a feeling your father is going to take care of something for Mid," Mrs. Bristol said. "Mid's safe for now. Let's clean up the basement."

What had taken a little monkey a short

time to do took Mrs. Bristol and Barbara a long time to clean up.

At last Barbara looked around. The tools were back in place. The spilled paint had been cleaned up. The soap had been swept away, and the clothes were back in the basket.

"I guess you'd never know a monkey had been busy here," Mrs. Bristol decided. "But I don't want another clean-up job."

It was almost lunchtime. As Barbara and Mrs. Britsol went into the kitchen they heard a whistle. It was "Bobwhite! Bobwhite!"

"There's your father," Mrs. Bristol said. "Open the door for him."

Barbara ran to help her father. He had books in one arm and a roll of wire netting under the other. It was the wire netting used to make chicken yards. A box of nails was in one pocket. A little padlock was in another.

Barbara said, "We found Mid. She's in her box right now."

"Good," said Mr. Bristol. "You'll have to look after her this afternoon. It will take me a while to build her house."

Mr. Bristol put down the wire netting, the box of nails, and the padlock. He took the books and started off for his workroom, where he drew plans for houses.

Nancy looked surprised.

"You're not going to make Mid's house first?" Nancy asked.

"First things first," Mr. Bristol said. "An architect has to do things in order. First he has to learn about who is going to live in the house he's planning."

"That's what the books are for," Barbara said. "You found some books in the library about monkeys."

"Right. I have read part of what they say already. I have a few ideas. Now I am going to try some drawings."

36

He fastened a piece of paper to his drawing board. He took a sharp pencil and a ruler. He began to whistle bobwhite to himself.

Barbara tiptoed out of the workroom. Her father liked to work alone. As she started down the hall she heard him say "A monkey house, hmmm. A monkey architect! Now let me see—" He sounded happy. Barbara smiled.

Mr. Bristol came down for lunch. Then he went out. He walked over to the neighbor on one side of the Bristols' home. Then he went to the other neighbor.

"Now what?" Barbara wondered.

"I can't imagine," Mrs. Bristol said. "But I am sure it's something for the house for Mid."

"Here comes Daddy," Nancy called. "Guess what Mrs. Winter gave him? A bushel basket!"

Mr. Bristol laughed at all the curious

faces as he walked through the kitchen and down to the basement.

Barbara took Mid out of the hatbox and held her while Mr. Bristol began to use his tools at his workbench.

First he took the metal top off an old kitchen table. It had been stored in the basement. Then he cut four pieces of wood. They were each exactly five feet long.

After that, Mr. Bristol took some plywood. He cut it to fit the size of the table top.

Barbara hadn't seen the plan for Mid's house. She tried to guess what her father was going to make.

Tim and Nancy ran off to play. Mrs. Bristol went marketing. But Barbara waited. Perhaps she could help.

"If you keep the basement door closed," Mr. Bristol said, "Mid can be free for a while. Then you can be my assistant."

Barbara put Mid down and she scampered to the top of a furnace pipe. She played hide-and-seek, watching the two giants who were making her house.

Mr. Bristol drew a round circle twelve inches across on the piece of plywood. With his electric saw he cut around the circle. Barbara didn't think the circle could be a door. It was too big.

"Hand me the two boards, Barbara," Mr. Bristol said. He measured them and cut them the same length.

The noise of the saw scared Mid at first. She hid, then she made a fast chattering sound.

"Mid's house has to be large enough to let her play in it," Mr. Bristol said. "If it's too small, it won't be a good home for her."

"Her cage at the pet shop was too little," Barbara said. "I felt sorry for Mid in it. She looked so sad."

"I think she'll like this. But it's too big

to put together here in the basement."

"I guess you'd never get it through the door," Barbara agreed.

"Right. Now watch Mid and help me carry these things out to the garage. I'll need my hammer and screwdriver. Maybe a drill."

Soon Barbara and Mr. Bristol had the plywood, table top, and the other pieces of wood in the garage. Mid seemed quiet and safe inside. No mischief yet!

Mr. Bristol got the wire netting, the bushel basket, and some rope. Barbara still couldn't guess why he wanted the basket, but she waited.

The busy sound of hammering filled the garage. The house for Mid began to take shape. The metal table was the floor. It would be easy to keep clean.

The plywood with the round hole went on top. A door in the top of the cage didn't seem right to Barbara, but still she waited.

40

Mr. Bristol made two smaller holes in the top. He knotted one end of the rope and dropped the other end down through the second hole.

Barbara clapped her hands. "A swing for Mid! Oh, thank you!"

Mr. Bristol stood back and smiled. The cage was beginning to look like the drawing he had on his drawing board.

When Mrs. Bristol got home, she came out to watch the work.

"I've got something for Mid, too," she said. "I'll just keep it for now."

Mr. Bristol put two boards like shelves at the sides of the cage. Then he made a small door near the floor of the cage. It was hinged to open easily.

Reaching in his pocket, Mr. Bristol pulled out the padlock.

"This is important. I read that monkeys are quick to learn how to get out of their cages. You have to have a lock. Some of

41

the big apes can open a lock if they find the key."

"I'll find a safe place for the key," Barbara promised.

"And I'll keep this extra one, just in case."

Mrs. Bristol walked around the cage. Now Mr. Bristol was stretching the wire netting across the four sides. He pulled it and tacked it. Barbara helped.

"It's fine. But why the hole in the top?" Mrs. Bristol asked.

"I'm glad somebody asked me about that. I was waiting," Mr. Bristol said. "It's the best part. And it's my own idea. Barbara, hand me that bushel basket."

While Barbara and Mrs. Bristol watched, the basket was fitted over the round hole. It made a dome on the top of the cage. Mr. Bristol nailed it in place.

"There! Mid will be the only monkey with a penthouse. You know a penthouse is a little house on top of a big building. I read that monkeys like a place to hide, and that is what Mid's penthouse is for."

"What a good idea!" Barbara said.

"Where are we going to put Mid's cage?" asked Mrs. Bristol.

"In this warm summer weather I think Mid will be fine outdoors. I thought I'd put her cage in a tree. I'll hang it with ropes so that we can pull it up and down."

Mrs. Bristol nodded. "That's good. We don't want Nancy's little friends poking fingers into Mid's house."

Barbara looked at the cage from every side. "If Mid has a penthouse," she said, "there should be a patio, too. I know! Those two shelves are her patios. Now, do you think she'll really like it?"

Mr. Bristol said, "There is only one way to find out if an architect has done good work. Somebody has to live in the house. Now is the time."

Just then Louise and Jean came home from work. Tim and Nancy ran into the backyard. The whole Bristol family was there.

Barbara went down to the basement. She called, "Mid, Mid, come here."

But Mid just looked down from the furnace pipe where she was sitting. It was her favorite place.

"What can we do?" Barbara asked. "Mid just won't come down."

Mrs. Bristol called, "Barbara, I have something in the kitchen that will help. Here."

"That's what I need!" Barbara said, and then she coaxed Mid. "I have something you like. Come and get it."

Barbara held out a yellow banana for Mid to see.

Mid peeked out. She saw the banana. She began to chatter. With a swing and a jump she was in Barbara's arms.

"Wait!" Barbara said. "You can have your treat in your new house."

Barbara carried Mid out to the garage. She put the monkey down and handed her father the banana. He put it in the cage.

Everyone stood still and waited. Mid looked at the cage. She saw the banana. She saw the open door.

Mrs. Bristol held her breath. Would Mid go in the cage by herself? She need not have worried. Mid didn't waste time. She was hungry.

As soon as Mid was inside, Mr. Bristol closed the door and snapped the lock.

Nancy started to say, "Nobody peeled the banana for Mid..."

"Nobody needs to. Look!" Barbara said.

Mid sat on one of her patios. She held the banana in one hand. She stripped the peel off, just the way a person would. Then she ate it.

Mid looked around. Did she know this

house had been built for her? She began to explore it.

The Bristols watched. One minute Mid was on the floor of her cage. Next she was running up the wire netting, holding on with fingers and toes. Up she went, right through the round hole and into her penthouse.

"See?" Mr. Bristol said. "I thought she'd like that."

Mid liked the penthouse so well, in fact, that no one could get her to come out.

"She's a girl all right," Mr. Bristol said. "She's just like every one of you. She wants a little place where she can be by herself."

The girls looked at each other and laughed. It was true. Every one of them had a special spot to read or write letters or listen to music. Even Louise and Jean.

4 GRANDMA MEETS Mid

Mid's first night in her new house passed safely.

Barbara was watching Mid play in her cage in the backyard. The telephone rang.

Everyone else was away, so Barbara ran in the house to answer.

"Hello," Grandma Bristol's voice said. "I thought no one was going to answer."

"I was out in the yard looking at our monkey," Barbara explained.

"Monkey? Did you say monkey?" asked Grandma Bristol. "I thought you said monkey."

48

"Grandma, I did! We have a pet monkey. Her name is Mid."

"And your father and mother are letting you keep her?"

"Yes, and Daddy made Mid a special house. Oh, Grandma, come and see it."

For a moment Grandma did not say anything. Then she said, "I'm having my hair washed and set in a new way. I'm calling from the Lady May Beauty Shop. I'll stop on my way home and meet Mid."

"That's wonderful, Grandma," Barbara said. "I'll be looking for you."

Barbara put the phone down. Now she began to wonder. Would Grandma Bristol like Mid? Of course she liked the other pets in the family, Pat and Kelly. But everyone always likes cats and dogs for pets.

"Well," Barbara told herself, "it's hard not to like Mid. But I hope she is good. If she gets into mischief—"

It was not long before Barbara heard Grandma Bristol's "Yoohoo, is anyone home?"

"Grandma, you look beautiful!" Barbara said. "Oh, I like your hair like that."

"You do? One of my friends is having a party this afternoon. I thought having my hair fixed a new way would give everyone something to talk about."

Barbara loved her grandmother. She was always saying funny things like that.

"Now where is this monkey? You didn't tell me you had a monkey just to get me to stop by, did you?"

"Mid is in the backyard," Barbara said. "Do you want to leave your things in the house?"

"No, I can't stay long. And besides, I have something for Mid. You know I always bring something when there's a new member in the family."

Barbara smiled. "Grandma, you're just

like Daddy. Nothing ever really surprises you. And you always think of something nice to do."

Grandma Bristol laughed. "Well, I'd say your father is like me, since he's my son."

Out in the backyard, Grandma Bristol looked at the cage. She waited until Mid peeked down from her penthouse.

"She is fun," Grandma Bristol said. "Look at those little hands. And how quick she is."

Barbara told her grandmother about the fire at the pet shop and why Mid needed a home.

Grandma Bristol walked all around the cage. Then she opened the paper bag she had with her. She took out a ripe peach.

"I know monkeys like fruit," she explained. "I thought perhaps your new pet would like a treat."

Standing close to the cage, Grandma Bristol held the peach toward Mid.

51

Mid scampered down and began to chatter.

"It's for you," Grandma Bristol laughed. "Come on." She bent closer to the wire netting. Barbara watched, smiling.

Suddenly Mid leaned over and pushed a little hand quickly through the netting. But she wasn't reaching for the peach. No! It was Grandma's silvery hair she wanted.

Grandma was still offering the peach as Mid pulled a curl. Mid's fingers caught in another curl. Before Grandma could back away, Mid had made a big change in how Grandma's hair looked. Her curls tumbled down, all out of place.

"Oh, Mid, you bad little monkey!" Barbara scolded. "Grandma, I'm so sorry. Oh, dear."

Grandma patted her hair and began to laugh. "Mid, you are a monkey. I don't like my hair when the curls are all so

tight. Now you've made me comb it out."

So Grandma Bristol fixed her hair, and Barbara agreed it looked nicer than it had before.

Using a knife, Grandma cut a slice of peach and gave it to Mid. This time she kept out of Mid's reach.

Barbara and Grandma Bristol were laughing at Mid's housekeeping when Mrs. Bristol came home. Mid threw out the peach pit and a peeling she didn't like.

"Mid's quite a pet," Grandma Bristol said.

"I'm glad you have met," Barbara's mother said. "I was afraid you'd think we were silly to let Barbara keep Mid."

"Not at all. Besides, Mid has given me a lot to talk about at my party this afternoon." And Barbara and Grandma Bristol laughed again about Mid's mischief.

As Grandma Bristol turned to go she

said, "There's one thing I wonder about. How do Kelly and Pat like Mid?"

"We really don't know," Barbara said. "So far they have left her alone."

"Just watch," Grandma Bristol said. "Pets are a lot like people. You know how older children in a family feel about a new baby. Sometimes they are cross and jealous."

"That's right," Mrs. Bristol said. "I hadn't thought about that. We'll have to pay more attention to Pat and Kelly."

"Bye-bye, Mid," Grandma Bristol called. "Be a good girl. Don't tease Pat and Kelly."

5 A Joke on Mid

It was Saturday evening a week later. The Bristols and their neighbors, the Winters, were having supper together in the backyard.

"I love sweet corn, don't you?" Nancy asked Mrs. Winter. She had just had her third piece.

"How about Mid? Does she like sweet corn?" Mrs. Winter asked.

Mrs. Bristol looked surprised. "Why, I don't know. We never gave her any."

Barbara said, "She likes fruit and vegetables. Let's try."

She got up from the picnic table and ran over to Mid's cage. She held out a small ear of corn.

It was too big to go through the wire netting, so Barbara opened the door. Mid took the corn. Then faster than anyone had expected, she ate it.

"Where did the corn go?" asked Nancy. "Nobody can eat corn that fast!"

The two families laughed. Mid eating sweet corn was a funny sight.

"Wait here," Mr. Winter said. "I have something I'd like to try."

Barbara looked at her father. She knew how much Mr. Winter liked to play jokes.

"He won't try to trick Mid, will he?"

"He did have that kind of look in his eye," Mr. Bristol agreed.

Mr. Winter came back. He walked over to the open door of Mid's cage. "Here," he said. "See what you can do with this." He held out an egg.

With a quick grab, Mid took the egg. It happened so fast Mr. Winter didn't have time to blink.

Up the side of her cage and to one of her patios Mid went.

"By the way," Mr. Bristol asked. "Is that egg hard-boiled?"

When Mr. Winter shook his head, Barbara said, "Oh, Mid, be careful."

Now everyone had the feeling you get when you watch a circus performer on a tightrope. What would happen to the egg?

Mid held the egg up to her nose. No smell. She passed it from one hand to the other. She found the egg too big and too smooth to bite. Her actions seemed to say, "What shall I do with this?"

Barbara begged, "Give me the egg. Please, Mid, give me the egg."

Then it happened. The egg slipped out of Mid's hands. When she tried to catch it, the egg broke.

There Mid sat, a broken egg shell in each hand, egg running down her chest.

The monkey looked from one hand to the other. Then she stuck out her tongue and tasted a bit of the egg inside one shell. Mmmm, she liked the taste.

Mid ran a finger around the shell, trying to get every bit of the sticky raw egg.

Now the joke was on Mr. Winter. He had thought she wouldn't like the egg. But she did.

Mid dropped the empty egg shells. Suddenly she found the egg on her chest. How could she get it into her mouth? Her hands weren't much help. And her tongue wasn't long enough to reach her chest no matter how she tried.

Then Mid found a way. She looked like a little child in a big sweater. She bent her head down as far as she could. Using her hands, she pulled at the loose skin on her chest. At last! She could lick off the egg she liked so much.

When everyone began to laugh, Mid made a dash for her penthouse. No more tricks on her for a while, she seemed to be letting them know.

After cleaning up the picnic table, the Bristols and their friends sat in the backyard, visiting.

"How about Pat and Kelly—do they like Mid?" Mr. Winter asked.

"That's what Grandma Bristol wanted to know, too," Barbara said.

Mrs. Bristol said, "Well, at first Pat and Kelly didn't pay much attention to Mid. But she was out of her cage today and I saw her tease Pat."

"You did?"

"You know how a cat sits still, but its tail moves? Mid was behind Pat. She saw that white tail of his moving back and forth, back and forth. She made a grab for it. You should have seen Pat jump.

I laughed. I just couldn't help it."

"Oh, Mother," Louise said. "You hurt Pat's feelings. No wonder he's been sulking."

Tim called, "Here, Pat, here, kitty." But no big white cat came.

"Where's Kelly?" Louise asked next. "Pat and Kelly are always together."

Mr. Bristol cleared his throat. He whistled "Bobwhite! Bobwhite!" But the pets did not come running.

Mid peeked out of her penthouse, but no one was looking her way.

Now Jean began to worry. "If Pat and Kelly have run off somewhere it's because of Mid. Barbara, sometimes I wish you had never brought that monkey home."

Mrs. Bristol felt having Mid was partly her doing as well as Barbara's. She jumped up from her lawn chair and said, "Oh, I'll call Pat and Kelly. I have a trick or two myself."

Going into the house, Mrs. Bristol took the food dishes for the pets. She filled each. Then she set the dishes down. She called, "Want to eat?"

Out from under the porch came Pat. He looked like a white streak. From behind the garage came Kelly, two long jumps behind the cat.

"Everything's all right," Mrs. Bristol said. "They're fine."

While all this was going on, no one saw Mid slip out of her cage. The door had been left open, and she moved so quietly and quickly she wasn't seen.

Now she sat at the edge of the flower bed. She seemed to be watching something. She did not move.

Barbara saw Mid—and then she saw Pat. There wasn't time to say anything. She could only watch.

Pat crept up behind Mid. The white cat moved without a sound. He never took his blue eyes off the monkey.

Bit by bit, Pat inched toward Mid. Barbara couldn't move. By now the rest of the family watched, too. Even Mr. Winter was still.

What would Pat do? Was he trying to get even with Mid for scaring him?

Pat crouched, ready to spring. Nancy was about to cry out when Pat pounced.

Pat's paws were ready to catch and hold Mid. But he landed on nothing but empty air!

Mid must have known Pat was creeping up behind her. As the cat pounced, she took off. She ran on all four legs. No cat could catch her!

Then before the watchers knew what had happened, it was Mid who was chasing Pat. Kelly, not to miss the fun, ran after the cat and the monkey.

Through the backyard the pets raced. Pat tried to get to his special hiding place.

A small hole under the porch led to it.

But the first time around, Mid was too close to Pat. He could not dive into his hole. Around the house the animals went again. This time the Bristols and the Winters were on their feet, laughing and cheering.

"Go, Pat," Tim cried.

"Catch him!" Mr. Winter called to Mid.

"Get them," Mr. Bristol told Kelly.

Somehow Pat got just far enough ahead of Mid to reach his hole under the porch. He disappeared from sight. Mid stopped short. She wasn't much bigger than Pat.

But the hole was too small. She could not get in. At last she gave up.

Kelly gave one last bark and went over to Louise.

"Good old dog," she said, and he lay down at her feet.

Mid climbed up the porch, swung over into the elm tree, and then down into her cage. She seemed to be telling everyone that she didn't care about cats and dogs. She could take care of herself.

"Mighty Mid," Barbara laughed.

But the next day it was a different story. Mid was out of her cage. She climbed into a tree where two blue jays had a nest.

Suddenly there was a terrible chattering from Mid. There were cries from the birds. Their shrill calls of "Stop thief! Stop thief!" filled the backyard.

A very frightened monkey came leaping out of the tree. She headed for the safety of her cage. Blue wings fluttered after her, diving down.

Mid dashed into her cage and up into her penthouse. No one could coax her out.

"She must have been trying to steal an egg from the blue jays' nest," Mrs. Bristol guessed. "She liked that egg Mr. Winter gave her."

"Yes, but she doesn't like blue jays," Barbara said.

And ever after that, even a butterfly flitting through the mesh of her cage would send Mid scrambling for safety to her penthouse.

"Mighty Mid, indeed," laughed Mrs. Bristol.

66

6 Mid Tries Painting

Barbara came in the house after feeding Mid.

"Summer vacation—it's the best time of the year," she told her mother.

"I thought you were going to work part of the time this summer," Mrs. Bristol said.

"I was, but I guess you'd say my job went up in smoke," Barbara answered.

Mrs. Bristol laughed and said, "Maybe you'll go to the store for me. I need eggs and milk."

Barbara didn't mind an errand. She waved at Mr. Winter as she passed his house. He was up on a ladder, painting the trim near the roof.

"How do you like it?" he called down.

"Fine," Barbara answered.

"We have to get everything ready," Mr. Winter said. "Big things are going to happen here soon."

"Oh?" Barbara asked.

Mr. Winter was glad to rest and talk.

"Yes, there's going to be a wedding here. Rosemary wants to come home to be married right here in our yard. A summer wedding."

"I think that's lovely," Barbara said. She started to go on. If she talked too long, her mother would begin to wonder where she was.

As she walked down the block, Barbara thought about Rosemary Winter. She had been away all summer. Rosemary had said once that if she and Dick had a big wedding, Nancy could be a flower girl.

Barbara smiled to herself. Just thinking about Nancy dressed up as a flower girl made her smile. Nancy was sure to do something funny.

Eeeeeek! The sound of brakes and a car bumping the curb made Barbara jump. She looked around in surprise.

An old car jolted to a stop. A very pale man looked out of the driver's window.

"Believe me—I saw it! I really did see it!" he said. "Nobody will believe me."

Another car pulled up at the curb.

"Anybody hurt? What's the matter?"

The driver of the first car was still shaking his head. "You won't believe this. I don't believe it myself. A monkey was following that girl."

"A monkey? You're kidding!"

"I'm not. I wasn't going fast. I was so surprised I just drove up the curb. I saw a monkey right here on Park Place."

When Barbara heard the word 'monkey'

she began to move back. If she could just get out of the way before anyone saw her it would be fine. Besides, one look up into the tree told her she was being watched. Brown eyes in a wrinkled little face stared down at her.

"That monkey was running along just like a dog. You have to believe me."

The second driver called out, "You, over there. Did you see a monkey?"

"Oh, oh," Barbara thought. Aloud she asked, "You mean me? No, I didn't see the monkey. But I guess it belongs to my family. It's a pet—"

"You see? I was right," the first driver said. "I wasn't seeing things. I feel better."

"A pet monkey?" the other man said. "Well, that's a new one." He shook his head and got into his car. Both cars left. Soon Park Place was empty again.

Barbara looked up at Mid. "You naughty monkey! Mid, you could have caused an accident. What are we going to do with you? Go home!"

Maybe Mid understood. At least she must have known Barbara was angry with her.

Mid swung from the branches of one tree to the next, down the street toward the Bristol house. Barbara stood watching her.

Mid had grown tame, and the Bristols did sometimes let her play outside her cage. But this was the first time she'd ever followed Barbara away from the yard.

"Should I go home and tell Mom?" Barbara wondered. "She'll fuss. I'm sure Mid will go and hide in her cage. I'll get the milk and eggs. Then I'll look after Mid."

So Barbara ran toward the store.

With the eggs and milk in a bag, Barbara started home. She thought again about what Mr. Winter had told her. She said to herself, "Just wait until I tell

Louise and Jean. I know some news before they do."

She crossed the street to her own block. "If it's going to be a garden wedding, maybe all of us will be invited," she thought, feeling happy.

She was almost in front of the Winters' house when she heard Mr. Winter.

"Come back here, you rascal! Come here, I say!"

In a flash Barbara knew. More trouble. She was afraid to look.

"Bring that paintbrush back!" Mr. Winter was shouting now.

Barbara wanted to run back toward the store. How could that one little monkey get in the middle of so much trouble so fast?

Mr. Winter's voice changed. He was trying something new. "Come on, Mid," he called in a sweet tone. "Look, I have something for you. A cookie! Come on, Mid.

That's a good monkey. Bring me the brush."

Barbara looked up. Mr. Winter was still at the top of the ladder. Just out of his reach was Mid. She had his paintbrush. Spots of paint dripped from the brush onto the roof of the house.

"You monkey, you!" Mr. Winter roared. Begging didn't do any good. Shouting at least made him feel better.

Now there was a new voice. Mr. Bristol ran into the Winters' yard.

He took one look and stopped. "Mid!" he called. Then he did a surprising thing. He whistled "Bobwhite!" just the way he did for Pat and Kelly.

Mid looked down. Maybe she thought that whistle meant a different kind of fun. She dropped the paintbrush. Off she ran over the top of the roof and down on the other side.

There was a big tree there. She swung

74

down into the Bristols' backyard. She saw Pat and Kelly coming at a trot to answer Mr. Bristol's whistle. In a flash she was in her cage, hiding in her penthouse.

Barbara didn't wait to be told what to do. Putting down the milk and eggs, she ran to the back of the house and pushed the cage door shut.

Click went the padlock.

"No more mischief for you, Mid!" she cried.

Then Barbara ran back to the Winters' yard. Mr. Winter was at the bottom of the ladder. Mr. Bristol was climbing up, a rag and a tin can in his hand. There was a paint cleaner in the can. Mr. Winter used it to clean his brush.

Mr. Bristol called down, "The paint is so fresh I can get most of it off. Just hold on to the ladder, will you?"

Mr. Winter called, "Glad to. I like being down on the ground. Whew! I was never meant to be a house painter."

Mr. Bristol rubbed away at the spilled paint. It didn't all come off, but it wasn't too bad.

Then Mr. Bristol came down and got the paint and brush. Pretty soon he was painting away for Mr. Winter.

"You know, I like this house painting. It's better than house planning."

Later Barbara told her father, "I think Mid gets both of us in the middle of trouble. What do you think she'll do next?"

Mr. Bristol laughed. "Who knows? When you have a monkey in the family you just have to wait and see. I'm sure it won't be long."

7 What Will the Neighbors Say?

When Louise and Jean came home from work, they heard the whole story about Mid's newest adventures.

Louise said, "Mother, if that monkey spoils Rosemary's wedding, I don't know what we'll do."

"Yes," agreed Jean. "Mid is just too much. Do you know what Mrs. Coleman down the block asked me yesterday?"

Mrs. Bristol looked at Barbara, and Barbara gave her a half smile. What next?

Jean said, "Mrs. Coleman asked me if our monkey likes to eat bread."

"Bread?" asked Nancy. "Mid doesn't like bread. What a funny idea."

"It isn't funny," Jean said. "Mrs. Coleman was having her order from the supermarket sent out. The truck stopped in front of her house. While the driver brought in the groceries, Mid helped herself to a loaf of bread from someone's order."

"She did?" exclaimed Mrs. Bristol. "How did Mrs. Coleman find out? Did she see Mid do it?"

"I guess not," Jean said slowly. "But Mrs. Coleman's neighbor, Mrs. Dale, did. She said Mid ran off with the bread under one arm, just like a person."

"So you see," said Louise, "the whole neighborhood thinks Mid is trouble."

"I see," said Mrs. Bristol sadly. "We are going to have to keep Mid in her cage. I guess that's all there is to it."

"Poor Mid," exclaimed Tim. "She can't

help being a monkey. That's just what she is."

At dinner Mr. Bristol looked around the table. "Want to hear another story about Mid?" he asked.

Jean and Louise looked at each other. They didn't have to say what they were thinking. Barbara could guess.

Tim and Nancy began to smile. They didn't understand the trouble Mid might be in.

"I just hope it isn't too bad," Mrs. Bristol said.

"Well, it's funny anyway," Mr. Bristol answered. "Bill Conway told me. He had a boy come to cut his grass last Saturday. The boy brought his lunch along to eat at noon."

"That's Steve," Tim said. "I know him."

Mr. Bristol went on, "Steve had his lunch in a brown paper bag. He tucked the bag into a tree to keep it out of reach of the Conways' dog. Steve saw Mid watching him, but he didn't worry about that. He likes Mid."

"So what happened?" asked Nancy.

"You know how curious Mid is. She had to see what was in that bag. Before Steve knew it, Mid grabbed the lunch bag. She scampered up to the highest branch of the tree."

"And?" Jean said.

"Mid got the bag open. She looked inside. She sniffed. She put a hand in and pulled out a sandwich. Off came the wrapping. She held the sandwich in her hands. She tried a little bite. It was lettuce. The first bite tasted good. Then she took a bigger bite."

Mr. Bristol stopped his story and laughed. "I can just see her! It was a baloney sandwich. This time she got some of the meat. A monkey won't eat meat. She couldn't spit it out fast enough. She

80

dropped the whole lunch bag and ran off."

"Did Steve have to go without his lunch?" asked Mrs. Bristol.

"No, Mrs. Conway fixed him a new sandwich. Steve said it was better than the one Mid dropped."

After dinner Barbara helped her mother clean up the kitchen.

"What are we going to do about Mid?" Barbara asked. "She's so funny, but she's so much trouble."

Mrs. Bristol sighed. "I guess we didn't know what having a monkey in the family would be like. She has to be kept in her cage. I don't know what else we can do."

"I guess you're right," Barbara said sadly.

For the next few days Mid chattered from her cage and begged to be let out. She scolded Pat and Kelly when they ran by where she could see them. They were free and she was caged.

One afternoon Tim looked up at Mid and said, "Yes, I know you want to be free. But if I let you out, we'll have trouble."

Mid didn't like that answer. She rattled her empty food dish on the metal floor of her cage. She ran from one side to the other. She swung on her rope swing. She shook the wire netting with her small, strong hands.

At last Tim put down the book she had been trying to read.

"All right, Mid," she said. "I'll take you out. But you'll have to go in the house. You are not going visiting down the block. Not today."

Tim opened the cage and took Mid in her arms. She carried her to the house. She was careful to shut the door behind her.

Now where was a safe place where Mid could play? Not the basement. Not the kitchen. Mrs. Bristol never let the monkey go in the kitchen.

Tim looked around. Not the living room. And the bedrooms would not do. And most certainly not Mr. Bristol's workroom.

The side porch had screens. That was the only place where Mid would be safe.

The telephone rang. Tim was the only person at home so she ran to answer it. She felt sure Mid would be all right on the porch.

Tim was away for hardly more than a minute. But when she came back to the porch, Mid was gone.

At first Tim hoped Mid was playing hide-and-seek with her. When Mid wanted to, she could be very quiet while everyone hunted for her.

After fifteen minutes of hunting, Tim was ready to give up. She left the porch and looked in the living room, the dining room, and the kitchen. Perhaps Mid had slipped past her when Tim went to answer the phone.

But Tim felt sure she had left Mid on the porch. Before going upstairs to look for the monkey, Tim went back to the porch.

This time Tim saw what had happened. One screen was a little loose. That was how Mid had escaped.

Tim asked herself what she should do. She could run all over the neighborhood looking for Mid and not find her.

The best thing, Tim decided, was to wait. "When Mid gets hungry or tired, she'll come home," she thought, hoping she was right.

Tim settled down with her book. It was a ghost story about an old house. She was just getting to the best part. She forgot all about Mid.

Then all at once Tim heard a scream. For a moment she thought that she had imagined it. Reading ghost stories can make you do that. But no—now there was another scream, and it was real.

Tim dropped her book. She didn't run away from the scream. She ran toward it. She was sure she knew the cause.

The scream came from the Colemans' backyard, at the end of the block. Tim took one look. She didn't know whether to laugh or cry. Clothes were dropped all over the ground in the Colemans' yard. What a sight!

Mrs. Coleman was trying to get a woman to stop crying.

Holding a clothespin in one hand and perched on an empty clothesline, Mid swung back and forth.

Tim made a flying leap and caught Mid before she knew she'd even been seen.

What Tim wanted to do was run home. But Mrs. Coleman caught sight of her.

"Come here!" she called. "Maybe Emma

will stop crying if you show that little monkey of yours to her."

Tim held Mid so that she couldn't get away. She walked slowly toward the Coleman house.

"See?" Mrs. Coleman said. "That's what you saw. My neighbors have a pet monkey —though I can't think why!"

Emma looked at Mid. It was a monkey. This was the first time she had worked for Mrs. Coleman. No one had said a word about a monkey.

Mrs. Coleman had said after lunch, "We'll hang out the winter clothes to air. It's a sunny day, and I like to hang them out in the sunshine."

So Emma had carried coats and mittens and sweaters to the backyard. She had filled one clothesline with winter clothes. She was just starting another. She didn't know what made her turn around, but she did. And that was when she saw

a small brown hand pull up a clothespin. A sweater fell to the ground.

Emma had not waited to see more. She screamed. She ran toward the house. She had no idea what was going on, and she was scared.

"Mrs. Coleman, I'm very sorry," Tim said. "Let me put Mid in her cage and I'll come back and help Emma."

Mrs. Coleman looked at Mid, who was still holding a clothespin, almost as if it were a banana.

"All right," she said. "I guess there hasn't been any harm done."

After Tim and Emma had all the winter things hanging in the sun Mrs. Coleman called to them. "Come up on the porch and have some iced tea."

While Tim drank her tea, Mrs. Coleman said, "I hear Rosemary Winter is going to be married soon. And the wedding is going to be outdoors, under the arbor."

"Yes'm," Tim said. "And my little sister Nancy is going to be the flower girl."

"You mean Mid isn't going to be in the wedding party?" Mrs. Coleman asked. "I don't believe anything can go on in this neighborhood that Mid doesn't get into."

Tim smiled, but she didn't think it was funny. She smiled just to be polite.

Mrs. Bristol was home when Tim got back. She heard all that had happened. Then she said, "Well, Mid is going to have about one more chance, I'm afraid."

"And then what?" asked Tim.

"I really just don't know," her mother said.

And when Louise came in she called, "Rosemary is going to be here tomorrow. The wedding is a week away."

8 Mid Goes to a Party

A call came from the backyard.

"Anyone home?"

Like popcorn, the five Bristol girls burst out of the house.

"Rosemary!" Jean and Louise said. Nancy ran to give Rosemary a hug.

"How about me?" Dick asked. He was the young man Rosemary was marrying. "Don't I get a hug?" He was like Rosemary's father. He liked to joke.

"We came over to meet Mid," Rosemary said. "Dad and Mom told us all kinds of stories about your new pet. Where is she?"

Barbara pointed to the cage hanging in the elm tree. Mid looked down at the people in the backyard just the way they looked up at her. She was curious.

Dick pulled some peanuts in the shell out of his pocket. He offered one to Mid. It was easy to see that Dick and Mid were going to be friends.

Rosemary and the two older Bristol girls began to talk about the wedding plans. After Dick had given his last peanut to Mid he said, "You girls won't miss me if I do some errands. Rosemary, I'll see you later."

Nancy asked Rosemary, "Am I really going to be your flower girl?"

"You are," Rosemary answered. "You'll have a long dress and flowers in your hair. You'll carry a basket of flowers to drop in front of Dick and me when we walk out to stand under the arbor."

"I can hardly wait," Nancy said.

Rosemary looked at Nancy's sisters. She said, "I'd like to have all of you in the wedding. You know that. But it's a garden wedding, and we want to keep it simple."

"But we can all come, can't we?" Tim asked, just to be sure.

"Yes! Even Mid can come if she likes," Rosemary answered.

"You don't know what you're saying," Barbara said.

Louise agreed. "I am afraid Miss Mid is sorry that she can't attend your wedding," she said.

Rosemary laughed. "Dick and I thought it would be fun years later to tell our children that a monkey came to our wedding."

"Maybe," Barbara said. She was only afraid that Mid would somehow come anyway without an invitation. Mid had a way of being in the middle of whatever was going on.

A busy time began for Mrs. Bristol and

Grandma Bristol. They cut out and sewed the long dress Nancy was to wear. It was trimmed with lace and flowers. Grandma Bristol made a circle of flowers for Nancy's hair.

The other girls chose their prettiest summer dresses to wear for the wedding.

Mr. Bristol and Mr. Winter went over the wedding plans, looking at the arbor and the garden.

The garden filled with late summer flowers would be a good background. The arbor with vines growing over it would give shade.

Mrs. Winter said, "I just hope it doesn't rain. It would spoil everything."

But Rosemary said, "Oh, Mother, we can have the wedding in the house. Please don't worry."

Mrs. Bristol said, "When I think of five daughters and five weddings, that's something to worry about."

Nancy saved some scraps from her dress. She found some little pieces of lace, too. She asked Barbara to help her. She thought it would be fun to make a little wedding outfit for Mid.

"Mid will feel left out," Nancy explained. "Maybe we can make her a fancy cape and a little bonnet."

Barbara laughed. She didn't think Mid knew or cared about the wedding. But it would be fun to make a special outfit for Mid.

So Barbara and Nancy worked in their bedroom and made a costume for Mid. Or at least they called it a costume.

"But Mid is not going to the wedding," Barbara said. "Just remember that, Nancy."

The day before the wedding, Barbara and Dick were playing with Mid. She was being a very good monkey and very funny. Everyone laughed at her and praised her.

94

Dick said, "You know, I think you should hang Mid's cage from a tree where the wedding guests can see it. I know one little boy who is coming, and he says he'd rather see the monkey than me."

"Yes," Rosemary said, holding Dick's hand. "I think Mid is part of the Bristol family. She should be nearby anyway."

So Mr. Bristol found a good place near the Winters' yard to hang Mid's cage. But Barbara and Nancy kept Mid's wedding costume a secret.

The day of the wedding came. The weather was just right. Rosemary was a beautiful bride. All the friends and the family at the wedding said everything was perfect. It was a lovely wedding.

A table was set with flowers, a white cloth, and the wedding cake. Everyone stood about talking until it was time for Rosemary to cut the cake. Dick would help her.

Nancy pulled Barbara's arm. She whispered, "Let's dress Mid in her costume. If we don't, it will be too late."

Barbara thought it didn't matter. But Nancy looked upset. She had been a very good little flower girl. Perhaps Barbara should do what Nancy wanted. Besides, Mid in her wedding costume would be a funny surprise for Rosemary and Dick. They would enjoy it.

Nobody missed Barbara and Nancy. Barbara quickly opened Mid's cage and took the monkey in her arms. Then the girls ran into the house.

Nancy brought the little cape the girls had made. She brought the wedding bonnet, too.

By this time, Barbara was wishing she was back at the party, not helping Nancy. Rosemary would be cutting the cake. She didn't want to miss that.

Hurrying made Barbara clumsy.

Mid was quick to take a chance when she found one. Before Barbara could do anything, Mid slipped out of her hands. She streaked across the porch and out the door, which was open a few inches.

"Oh, oh, oh!" was all Barbara could say. She shut her eyes. She didn't have to see Mid climb a tree near the fence of the Winters' yard. She knew what Mid would do.

Nancy chased after Mid. She held her long dress up as she ran. But she couldn't catch Mid.

Mid swung from the branch of the tree in the Bristols' backyard over to the vine-covered arbor. The wedding guests were too busy talking and laughing to notice her.

Dick was helping Rosemary cut the wedding cake. They shared the first piece. Now it was time to pass little sandwiches and cake to everyone.

Nancy looked around for Mid. She

couldn't find the monkey at all. But Nancy saw a man with a tray of sandwiches coming toward her under the arbor. She hoped he would stoop down to let her choose one. She was hungry.

As the man with the tray walked under the arbor, he saw Nancy. He asked, "Little girl, would you like—" But he stopped.

The man stared at the tray. Two brown, hairy arms, two tiny hands seemed to come from nowhere. They swept the tray clean of sandwiches! Not a sandwich was left!

From up in the arbor came a burst of fast chatter and monkey talk. Mid had come to the party!

Everyone began to laugh and point at Mid. Rosemary and Dick laughed, too. But Louise and Jean and Tim and Barbara looked ready to cry.

Mr. Winter said, "Don't worry. A little food is spoiled, that's all. Everyone is hav-

ing a good time. I guess Mid can have fun, too."

The little boy who had come to the wedding helped Barbara catch Mid. Then Barbara explained how Mid had had the chance to get out of her cage.

Rosemary said, "Lots of people are taking pictures. Why don't you put Mid's wedding cape and bonnet on her and bring her back? It would be fun to have a picture with the only monkey that ever came to a wedding."

"If we don't have a picture, no one will ever believe us," Dick said.

So Barbara and Nancy dressed Mid in her costume and brought her back.

In the book of pictures that Rosemary and Dick had of their wedding, the one they liked best to show had Mid in the center.

Dick always said, "You'd think it was Mid's wedding!"

9 Away for the Winter

The last of summer went by too fast. Nancy was glad when school began. But Barbara and Tim just said, "Homework!"

Mrs. Bristol looked around the empty house. No girls running in and out. No telephone calls. Nobody to keep her from doing her work.

Nobody but Mid.

Mid's cage hung from the elm tree in the backyard. Mrs. Bristol went out to take Mid some food.

"You miss the girls, too, don't you?" she asked Mid. "It's too quiet around here."

Mid ran around inside her cage. She played a game of hide-and-seek with Mrs. Bristol. She hid in her penthouse. Mrs. Bristol pretended she was going into the house. Then Mid ran down from the top of her cage. She took a swing, caught at the side of her cage, and chattered.

Mrs. Bristol laughed. "Yes, we both miss the girls, Mid."

One morning when Barbara was dressing for school she put on her new sweater. It was brown, like her hair.

"How nice you look," Mrs. Bristol said at breakfast. "Do you like the sweater Grandma knitted for you?"

"I do," Barbara answered. "It feels good on a chilly morning."

Mrs. Bristol frowned. She said, "I wish Grandma could knit a sweater for Mid. She's going to need something pretty soon. The weather is getting colder."

"I saw a pattern for a dog sweater," Tim

102

said. "Maybe Grandma Bristol could use that for Mid."

"Well, I don't really think so," her mother said.

Mr. Bristol was sitting at the breakfast table, too. He had not gone up to his workroom yet.

"When I made that cage, I knew it was too big to bring indoors. Hmmm. I wonder if I should make a new house—an indoor house—for Mid."

Barbara said, "It has to be big enough to let Mid play and move around."

"That's right," Mr. Bristol agreed. He looked thoughtful.

"Where would we put such a big cage?" asked Mrs. Bristol.

She looked around. "I wouldn't have it in the kitchen. I'm sure of that. And I wouldn't have it in the dining room."

"I can't imagine it in the living room," Tim said.

"How about our bedroom?" Nancy suggested.

Mr. Bristol said, "There's not enough room for you and Barbara and Tim. If I could make this house bigger, I'd give you and Mid all your own rooms."

Nancy laughed. "That would be fun."

Mr. Bristol went on. "Louise and Jean aren't going to share a room with a monkey. Neither are your mother and I. That leaves my workroom. I'm not ready to go into monkey business yet."

Mrs. Bristol laughed—she always laughed at Mr. Bristol's jokes. "But I don't know why I'm laughing," she said. "Mid has to have a winter home."

Barbara said, "Monkeys live in warm places. They aren't like bears. Bears sleep all winter."

Mr. Bristol looked at Barbara and asked, "Do you think the Midway Pet Shop would take Mid back?"

104

Mrs. Bristol and Barbara both said "NO!" at the same time. "Never."

"Well, perhaps you two can think of a way to send Mid to Florida or California for the winter," Mr. Bristol said. "And I wouldn't mind going, too."

"You girls run along," Mrs. Bristol said after looking at the clock. "You'll be late if you don't hurry."

That day at school Barbara decorated her papers with monkeys. She kept thinking about Mid and frost coming.

She thought maybe the Winters might take Mid. They had a big house and no children, now that Rosemary was married.

But the Winters liked to travel. They would not be able to keep a monkey, even if they wanted to do it.

Mrs. Bristol thought about Mid as she put away the breakfast dishes. She thought about her some more as she dusted in the dining room.

The dining room had a big sunny window. Mrs. Bristol kept her house plants there. When she watered them this morning she saw that one of the plants was wilted. It was her favorite African violet.

Mr. Bristol came downstairs from his workroom, and Mrs. Bristol showed him the violet.

"Take it to the doctor," he suggested.

Mrs. Bristol said, "Please, don't joke. I don't want this plant to die."

"I meant that," Mr. Bristol said. "That violet isn't too big to carry. So why not take it over to Joe Pace's greenhouse? I think he might tell you what to do for a sick plant. I'm sure he'll try."

Mrs. Bristol nodded. "I guess I will. I'll go after lunch. I can order some birthday flowers for Grandmother Bristol at the same time."

A greenhouse was one of the places that Mrs. Bristol always liked to visit. She liked the smell of the earth and growing plants. She liked the warmth and the sun shining through the glass walls. The ferns and other big plants helped her forget winter was coming.

Mr. Pace took Mrs. Bristol back into his greenhouse to pick out a plant for Grandma Bristol. She found a yellow one she thought was just right.

Mr. Pace looked at the African violet. He suggested what she could do for it.

Mrs. Bristol looked around. She asked, "What's that big plant over there? It can't be a banana plant, can it?"

"That's what it is," Mr. Pace said. "And there is something funny about it. It isn't mine. You might say I am giving it room and board for the winter months."

"You are?" asked Mrs. Bristol.

"Yes, the owners are going on a trip. None of their friends had a house big enough for a banana plant. So they asked

107

me to keep it for them until they come back."

When Mrs. Bristol got home, she walked out and looked at Mid.

"I wonder," she said to herself. "It might just be the answer."

At dinnertime, Mrs. Bristol brought up the problem about Mid and cold weather.

Mr. Bristol laughed and said, "I told you Mid should go to Florida."

"Oh, no," Nancy said, and Louise said, "Nancy, you know Dad is joking."

"Well, I'm not joking," Mrs. Bristol said. "And I think Mid should go somewhere that's warm all year around."

Barbara was shocked. "You mean that, Mom? You want us to send Mid to Florida?"

"No, not quite. I have another idea. And I don't even know if it will work."

"Tell us," everyone said.

"I went over to Joe Pace's greenhouse

this afternoon. And do you know what he is doing?"

Mrs. Bristol liked to make a story last. The family always said, "Go on, tell us."

"Joe Pace has a big banana plant he's keeping all winter in his greenhouse. The owners are away. They asked him to keep it for them. A banana plant has to have a warm place."

Barbara said, "Oh, Mom, I can guess!"

"And I thought maybe, just maybe, Mr. Pace could keep Mid for us in his greenhouse."

"That's not such a foolish idea," Mr. Bristol said. "Monkeys live in warm jungles. A greenhouse always makes me think of a jungle."

"And Mr. Pace's greenhouse is not too far away. We could visit Mid there," Tim said.

"I'll miss her," Barbara said. "But I guess it's a good idea."

"Will you talk to Joe Pace about it?" Mrs. Bristol asked her husband.

"How about tomorrow morning?"

"That would be fine."

Mr. Pace was certainly surprised. "You want *me* to take Mid for the winter?" he asked. "I'm a plant man, not an animal man."

Mr. Bristol said, "I know that. But Mid is healthy and not much care. Her cage could hang from the ceiling of the greenhouse. I even have an idea she'd be good for business."

"I suppose people would come in to see her," Mr. Pace said slowly. "And people who come in the greenhouse often buy plants before they go."

Mr. Bristol said, "Barbara will come over and help feed Mid and keep her cage clean, if that's all right with you."

"All right," Mr. Pace said. "We can try it. Perhaps it is a good idea."

110

And so that was how a winter home was found for Mid.

A cool breeze was blowing as Barbara helped her father with Mid's cage. It was too large to carry over to Pace's Greenhouse.

"I think we can fasten it on the roof of the car," Mr. Bristol decided. "I've carried other loads that way."

"I'll put Mid in her old hatbox," Barbara said. "She can ride inside with me."

Nancy wanted to be helpful. "I'll take Mid's food dishes," she offered.

Mid seemed to know that something was happening. She didn't seem scared, but she was quiet. Mrs. Bristol came out to say good-bye.

"Oh, you'll see Mid often," Mr. Bristol told her. "With Mid at the greenhouse, you'll have a good excuse to go and talk about African violets with Joe Pace."

It took some lifting and pushing to get

Mid's cage into the greenhouse. Mr. Pace had made a place for the cage not too far —and not too near—the banana plant.

Before the cage was in place, people began to ask questions.

"A live monkey? What fun!"

"I'll bring my little girl over to see it. May I?"

"What's the monkey called?"

Mr. Pace began to like the idea. He thought Mid looked right at home among all the tropical plants.

And Mid soon seemed to feel at home. Maybe she had never been in a jungle, but it seemed like the right place to her.

Children liked to come to see the monkey at Mr. Pace's greenhouse. They asked so many questions that Mr. Pace put up a sign.

The sign said, "I am a Rhesus monkey. My name is Mid. I belong to the Bristols. Please do not feed me."

10 Is It Good-bye?

For the first week or so the Bristols worried about Mid. Would she like her new winter home in the greenhouse? Would she miss getting out of her cage?

"Can we bring Mid home for a visit?" Nancy asked.

Mrs. Bristol thought about that. Then she said, "No, I feel it's better if Mid stays in one place. If she comes home, it will be hard to take her back."

Barbara said, "Besides, she might catch cold. Monkeys do that, you know. They

114

are a lot like people. Now she is used to the warm air in the greenhouse."

So Nancy said, "All right. But I can go along and say hello when you look after Mid, can't I, Barb?"

"You were my best monkey-helper right from the first day," her big sister said.

The winter days went by, and spring came. Mid was never lonely at the greenhouse. There were always people stopping by her cage to talk or play with her.

Mr. Pace sometimes laughed and said that Mid was his new partner. "And she isn't a silent partner," he would say.

"What does Mr. Pace mean?" Nancy asked.

Barbara said, "A silent partner owns part of a company but he keeps it quiet, sort of like a secret. It's hard to explain."

"Well, I know Mid isn't quiet," Nancy said. "She chatters a lot. I guess that's what Mr. Pace means."

The trees outdoors began to show new green leaves. Flowers started to grow in the Bristols' garden. Kelly lay on the back steps in the sun. Pat curled up beside him.

"When I have to step around that dog and cat, I know spring is coming," Mrs. Bristol said.

"How soon can Mid come home?" asked Barbara.

Mr. Bristol said, "When it's about as warm outside as it is inside the greenhouse. We don't want to have too big a change for Mid."

At last the weather seemed right. The Bristols and the Winters had a coming-home party the day Mid came back from Mr. Pace's greenhouse.

Nancy made a circle of spring flowers to put on the outside of Mid's cage. Mr. Bristol put a new rope swing inside the cage. Mrs. Bristol found new food dishes.

116

Pat and Kelly didn't seem too happy to have Mid home. They came and went as they pleased. Pat was always careful not to turn his back on Mid if she was out of her cage. Perhaps he remembered that wild chase around the house.

But when summer came, it seemed different from the summer before. Barbara was more grown up. She did a lot of baby-sitting. Tim did most of the things for Mid.

One afternoon Mrs. Bristol was sitting in the backyard near Mid's cage. She put her book down and looked up at the little monkey.

Mid was sitting in one corner of her cage. She wasn't swinging on her swing. She wasn't rushing about, up and down. A butterfly flew through the side of the cage. Last year, Mid would have hidden in her penthouse. This year she didn't seem to care.

Mrs. Bristol felt unhappy. There was

something sad about Mid in her cage. She tried to think what made this summer so different.

"Maybe it's because Mid is older, too," she thought. "Perhaps an older monkey isn't as full of play."

But somehow that did not seem the answer.

Grandmother Bristol stopped by to say hello. She looked up at Mid and offered her a bit of peach. Mid ate it, but she didn't try to grab Grandma's hair. She didn't even throw the peach pit out the way she once did.

Grandmother Bristol looked at Mid for a while. At last she said, "I have a feeling that Mid is unhappy."

"That's exactly what I think," Mrs. Bristol said. "But why?"

"Not enough going on," Grandmother Bristol said. "I know. I feel just the same way when nothing special is happening.

Then I go off and visit someone. Or I ask one of my old friends to come and have some tea."

"But Mid can't do that," Mrs. Bristol said. "She has to wait for someone to come. She was happy at the greenhouse. There was a lot going on there. But it's quiet here now."

She looked up at Mid in her cage.

Grandmother Bristol said, "I'll tell you something else. A monkey is a monkey. Don't laugh. A monkey isn't a person."

"I know that," Mrs. Bristol said. "But what do you mean?"

Grandma said, "Well, I like to visit you and the children. But you know I like to have my own friends, too. I mean people like me, who are my age."

Mrs. Bristol stood up. "Grandma, you're right! Now I understand what you're saying. Mid needs friends of her own kind. Monkey friends."

"That's what I think," Grandmother Bristol said.

At the dinner table that evening, Mrs. Bristol told the family what Grandma had said.

For a bit no one said anything. Not even Nancy. Then Barbara said slowly, "I think Grandma is right. But how do you feel about having another monkey? Then Mid wouldn't be lonely."

"Another monkey?" asked Louise. "One monkey is fine. Mid is fine. But two monkeys!"

Mr. Bristol shook his head. "You forget that Mid needed a home and that is why we got her. If we had to buy a monkey, we'd have to think about the cost. Monkeys cost a lot of money."

Mrs. Bristol shook her head. "I wasn't even thinking about buying *another* monkey."

"Then what?" asked Tim.

120

Jean looked at her mother and smiled. "I think I know. The place where there are a lot of monkeys is the zoo."

"But they don't give monkeys away at the zoo," Tim said.

"No, but maybe they take monkeys as gifts," Mr. Bristol said. "I think that's what your mother is trying to tell you."

Mrs. Bristol looked at her five girls and her husband. They were the dearest family in the world!

"Yes," she said. "That is what I was thinking. You all know that I wanted a monkey. I don't know why. I just did. When Barbara brought Mid home, I enjoyed having a monkey in the family. She was always in the middle of something, but it was fun. She had a good time, and we had a good time."

"But—" Barbara said.

"But," Mrs. Bristol said, "things change. You girls grow up. Mid grows older, too.

She is lonely. I don't think she misses you girls. She misses something she's never had. She misses other monkeys."

No one spoke. The idea of losing Mid was sad. Everyone would miss her.

Then Mr. Bristol said, "You know, we were happy to have Mid warm and comfortable at the greenhouse all winter. We knew that was best for her. Now I think we can be happy if we know the zoo is the best place for her."

Slowly Barbara nodded her head, and so did the others.

The next day, Mrs. Bristol drove to the zoo. She talked with some of the animal keepers. They showed her where the monkeys lived in the zoo.

"Will you—will you take a little tame monkey as a gift?" she asked.

At first she thought the zoo people were going to say that they would not. They said too many people wanted to give them

122

monkeys. But at last they agreed when they learned that Mid was healthy but lonely.

"Daddy, you take Mid to the zoo," Barbara said. "I think that's the best way."

And so it was agreed that Mr. Bristol would drive by himself with Mid to the zoo.

No one talked much about Mid for a few days after that. Then Mrs. Bristol said, "You know, Mid is fine. Why are we all so sad? Just think about how she stole Mr. Winter's paintbrush. That was a pretty funny trick. But I wouldn't want her to do it again."

"And how she chased poor Pat," Louise said. "I won't forget that."

"When can we go to see Mid?" asked Nancy.

Mrs. Bristol answered, "I think we have to give Mid time to feel at home at the zoo. It's like sending a child off to summer camp. If parents visit too soon, the child feels homesick."

So the Bristols decided to wait for a while before going to visit the monkeys at the zoo.

One Friday Mrs. Bristol said, "How about next Sunday afternoon? You'll all be home. Let's take a picnic lunch and go to the zoo. We can make it a family day."

Sunday was a perfect summer day. It was just the day for a picnic.

Barbara helped make sandwiches. Mrs. Bristol noticed that she was not looking happy. "What's the matter?" she asked.

"Oh, Mom," said Barbara. "I'm afraid. I'm afraid Mid won't know us. And we won't know her. It's so sad!"

"I have thought about that, too," Mrs. Bristol said. "Maybe Mid will be so happy with her own friends that she won't remember her human family. We'll just have to see."

124

At the zoo, Nancy ran ahead of the other Bristols down the path toward Monkey Mountain. She remembered the way from other summers.

The rest of the family hurried along after Nancy. Barbara was the last one. She kept wondering if Mid would remember her. And how would she know if Mid did remember her? One little monkey looks just like every other little monkey at the zoo.

"I didn't think there were so many monkeys," Mrs. Bristol said, shading her eyes to look at all the animals on Monkey Mountain.

Jean said, "I don't know which way to look first."

"Do you think Mid is really here?" Nancy asked. She was beginning to sound sad.

"Oh, I'm sure she is," Mrs. Bristol said. "We just have to find her."

For several minutes the Bristols stood and watched the monkeys.

"I was sure that was Mid," Louise said. She pointed at a monkey running off over the top of a rock. It was teasing another monkey.

"That monkey is too big," Jean objected. And Louise said, "That's what I thought when I looked a second time."

"Oh, dear," Barbara said. "I don't like this at all. I wish we hadn't given Mid away. We should have kept her."

Suddenly Nancy pointed at two monkeys high up on a bare branch of a tree on Monkey Mountain.

"Aren't they cute?" she asked. "Maybe one of them is Mid."

"Maybe," Tim said.

Then Mr. Bristol said, "Perhaps we can find out. Everyone watch closely—" And loud and clear, Mr. Bristol whistled "Bobwhite! Bobwhite!"

One little monkey, one of the two on the branch, began to chatter wildly. She ran down the tree and back and forth.

"Mid, here we are, here's your family!" Barbara called. "Oh, Mid, you haven't forgotten us!"

Mrs. Bristol smiled. "How could she?" she asked. "Mid was the monkey in our family."